Hong Kong History Girl

by Jane Houng

QX Publishing Co.

Hong Kong History Girl

Author: Jane Houng

Editor: Betty Wong

Illustrator: Tam Cheuk-man

Cover Designer: Cathy Chiu

Published by:

QX PUBLISHING CO.
8/F, Eastern Central Plaza, 3 Yiu Hing Road, Shau Kei Wan, Hong Kong
http://www.commercialpress.com.hk

Distributed by:
SUP Publishing Logistics (H.K.) Limited
3/F, C & C Building, 36 Ting Lai Road, Tai Po, N. T., Hong Kong

Printed by:
Elegance Printing & Book Binding Co., Ltd.,
Block A, 4/F, Hoi Bun Industrial Building, Hong Kong

Edition:
First edition, December 2018

ISBN 978 962 255 132 9

Printed in Hong Kong

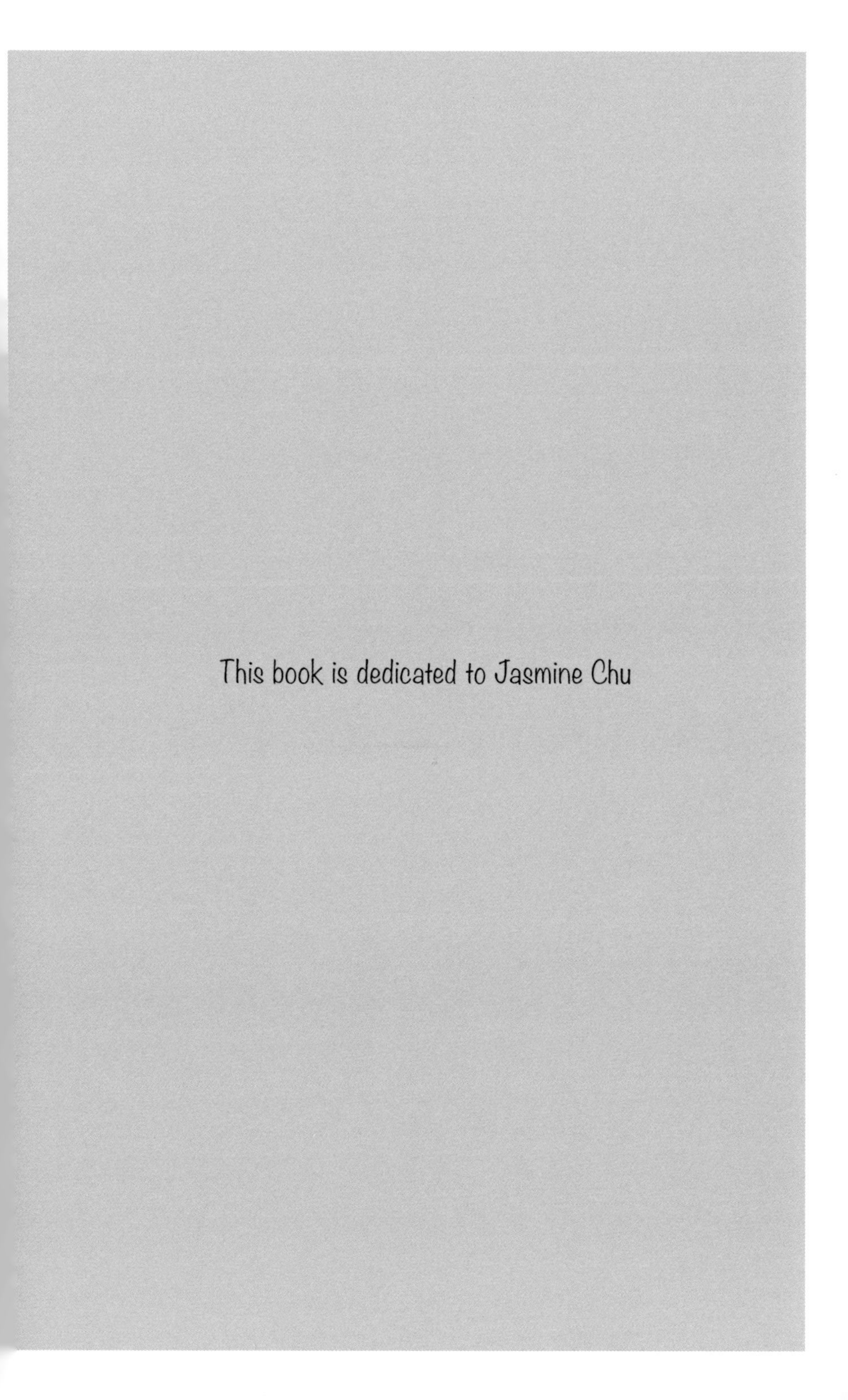

This book is dedicated to Jasmine Chu

Contents

Chapter 1

A Magical Surprise

One sunny afternoon Jasmine and Gong Gong Gramps were on the Hong Kong Ferris wheel, climbing higher and higher, high as hawks, when there was a rushing, a sucking, a watery WHOOSH, and they were standing beside a slab of rock.

'What happened?' said Gramps.

Jasmine tightened her bunches. She knew exactly where they were: Sung Wong Toi, Hong Kong's most ancient relic. A member of the crew with gold teeth and a curious hat, the one who'd winked as he opened the capsule door for them, had somehow spun them from Central to Kowloon City.

Jasmine recalled Teacher Tam handing her the instruction sheet of a summer holiday history project. 'I've planned a magical surprise for you,' he'd said, the day after finding her in the playground crying about Nai Nai being no more. 'Go to the Ferris wheel and someone will take you to the first site.' Since then, Gramps had moved into their flat. But Jasmine still missed her nai nai, a lot.

For the project, Jasmine had to visit eighteen sites. At each site she'd find a clue to the next location and one letter of a mystery message. Who'd have thought that Teacher Tam could make magic? Even the clouds seemed to be smiling!

Gramps was leaning on his stick near the

wall of a dry fountain, gulping air like a goldfish.

Jasmine pulled her funny face.

Gramps laughed, which warmed her heart. 'Check that history app or whatever you call it,' he said.

Jasmine cleared her throat and read. *'In 1279, a courtier jumped into the sea with the last Southern Song emperor, a boy, strapped to his back. They were escaping from the Mongols. Locals recorded this piece of history on a boulder. Many hundreds of years later, the boulder got in the way of building Kai Tak airport so a section was blasted away and erected here.'*

'Maybe the characters were carved by a great-gong gong of Nai Nai,' said Gramps sadly.

Ugh-oh. Jasmine ran over to give him a

Historical Site 1: Sung Wong Toi

hug. Cheering-up duty was hers when her parents were out at work.

'What's this?' Gramps's arm disappeared down the fountain wall.

Yeah! It was an envelope. Jasmine tore it open. Inside was one sheet of paper with typed Chinese characters. It must be the clue to the next site!

'Where are my glasses?' said Gramps,

fumbling in his shoulder bag.

But Jasmine was already reading aloud: *'The most ancient pagoda in Hong Kong.'*

A mystery letter was handwritten below that: it was the letter **I**.

Chapter 2

Divine Signs

Mr Crewman cocked his cap to shade his eyes but his teeth still flashed gold. He pulled a lever and the Ferris wheel slowed. 'Here you are: number eight,' he said.

The capsule rocked gently to and fro as it climbed higher and higher. Jasmine felt dizzy. 'Hold tight,' Gramps said, eyes closed, gripping her hand.

WHOOSH! They were at the Tsui Sing Lau Pagoda. The early-Ming three-storey building towered above them like a giant beehive. Stone phoenixes preened, dragons curled and fish splashed on its tiled roofs. 'Coming inside?' asked Jasmine.

The space was small, stuffy, hot. A red ladder led to the floor above. Jasmine reached for a rung but a security guard stopped her. She read from her app instead: '*Scholars and officials surnamed Tang were common in the Ming and Qing dynasties. A Ming dynasty Mr Tang wanted to build a pagoda here in order to scare evil spirits away and stop floods destroying crops. One night all the stars gathered and spilled like a waterfall to show him where to lay the first brick. Now, people come here to pray for good luck in exams.*'

Gramps straightened his back. 'Nai Nai was a Tang,' he said. 'You got your brains from her.'

Jasmine shrugged. Gramps had come to

Historical Site 2: Man Cheong Pagoda

Hong Kong on a leaky boat from Shantou.

The fiery eyes of two gods stared at Jasmine from a shrine. The statue on her right had an angry red face. It was Kwan Tai, the warrior god. The other, Man Cheong, the god of scholars, had a droopy moustache and held a pen. Peacock feathers bristled from his head. Jasmine bowed three times to each of them.

Where was the next clue? It couldn't be far.

Jasmine looked in all four corners of the pagoda.

Hurrah! There was a folded note behind Man Cheong's feathers. The clue was: *One of the largest ancestral halls in Hong Kong*.

The mystery letter was **H**.

Chapter 3

A Double Fast Spin

Grumpy Gramps was blaming his aching knees on the rain. How could Jasmine cheer him up? By taking him on a magical mystery tour! 'Guess where I want to go today,' she said.

Gramps shrugged. He was so boring sometimes.

Jasmine stood up. 'Tang Chung Ling Ancestral Hall, where Nai Nai played as a child.'

Gramps pulled one of her bunches. 'Good

girl,' he said.

They ate some pork noodles and set off. Luckily, the rain had stopped. In Central the Ferris wheel wasn't moving but Mr Crewman was standing on the platform as if waiting for them. 'New Territories, Fan Ling?' he said, 'No problem. I'll spin the wheel double fast.'

WHOOSH! Jasmine and Gramps landed in a yard surrounded by pot plants and sweet-smelling bushes. 'Look at that rainbow,' said Gramps.

The hall was a cheerful building with tall columns. Jasmine read about it from her app: *The main worship area is split into three. Each space displays rows of ancestral tablets.*

The tablets were stacked high on the wall like stone books. Jasmine recited the names: Tang Man Cheong, Tang Sze Lut, Tang King Yeung. So many famous Tangs!

Historical Site 3: Tang Chung Ling Ancestral Hall

'The most powerful clan in southern China,' boasted Gramps.

Jasmine looked for the tablet of Tang Si Meng, the servant revered for sacrificing his life for his master. She felt sure that the next clue would be hidden behind it. Oh no! It was right at the top in the middle. Far too high for her to reach.

'I think I can see it,' said Gramps. He was

leaning against the altar looking behind a stone frieze of a lively banquet scene. 'Come here!'

While the security lady wasn't looking, he lifted Jasmine. She put her elbows on the edge and grabbed the envelope.

'I can't find my glasses,' said Gramps.

Jasmine tore the envelope open.

Where was the next site? *'Also very far away from Central. It's a fort built in the Qing dynasty.'*

'And what's the letter?' said Gramps.

The next letter of the mystery message was **O**.

Chapter 4

An Abandoned Fort

Jasmine's history project was progressing well. She'd gathered information and images from the internet and typed up her notes from each trip. But would Teacher Tam's magic stretch as far as the western tip of Lantau Island? The next site was Fan Lau Fort.

Gramps was snoozing in his armchair with a framed photo of Nai Nai in his hand. Jasmine shook him awake and after a bowl of fish-ball noodles they travelled to Central.

When Mr Crewman smiled his eyes

scrunched into slits. 'Fan Lau? No problem,' he said.

Rush, suck, slobbery WHOOSH: Jasmine and Gramps were standing in a meadow listening to the sloshing of a restless sea. Remains of the fort rose from the ground like the foundations of a new tower block. '*It's 46 metres by 21*,' Jasmine said, reading from her history app. '*Built in 1729. Thirty soldiers lived here to stop pirates entering Hong Kong waters. They fired from eight cannons*. Look, here's one of them. BANG!' Jasmine did a star jump.

The fort had fallen into disuse after the pirates were defeated. Jasmine imagined a time when it was completely hidden. She'd read about an adventurer who'd studied a Qing dynasty book and calculated where it must be. Then he'd hired a sampan to reach this remote spot, hacked through the undergrowth and

Historical Site 4: Fan Lau Fort

unearthed it.

Jasmine looked at a seabird through her telescope. It swooped through the air searching for food.

'What's that over there?' said Gramps, walking towards a plaque. At its base was a mound of dirty old bricks. An envelope peeped out from under one of them. It must be the next clue! Jasmine ran over.

'A famous pirate's cave,' she read. 'I know! Cheung Po Tsai's cave, on Cheung Chau Island,' she exclaimed.

'Don't forget to make a note of the next letter,' said Gramps.

It was the letter **P**.

Chapter 5

Treasure Hunting in Cheung Chau

A black-bearded pirate waving a cleaver woke Jasmine up. She'd been on a beach, run, run, running but he was catch, catch, catching up. She could feel his breath on her neck. 'Help!' she cried.

Her parents had already left for work and Gramps was in the kitchen cooking morning *congee*. 'Anything wrong?' he called.

Jasmine ran to him. She wrapped her arms around his waist while he sprinkled handfuls of fish glue and fungus over the bubbling rice porridge. Mmm, it smelled delicious. 'Five minutes,' he said.

Jasmine dressed in her favourite pink dress. Why was it her favourite? Because it matched her bunches perfectly.

Gramps slurped his congee. 'I bet no one has told you. Your great-great grandpa was a pirate,' he said. 'In Qing times, hundreds of them prowled local waters. Fights and raids were common. Little girls like you needed gramps like me to take care of them.'

Jasmine shivered. How lucky she was to be living in the twenty-first century. Her home was safe from pirates. And she could travel from Ho Man Tin to Mr Crewman by MTR.

On the way, Jasmine read about Cheung Po Tsai on her app: *... leader of the Red Banner fleet. He became so rich that his cave wasn't big enough to store all his treasure. It's*

Historical Site 5: Cheung Po Tsai's Cave

rumoured that there's a secret entrance to a second cave.

The Ferris wheel was packed with holiday-makers queuing for capsules. *Creak!* Jasmine and Gramps were climbing. Jasmine wondered if it was only capsule number eight that was magic when – WHOOSH! – they'd landed on Cheung Chau.

Jasmine and Gramps followed signs to the

cave, holding hands through a scary cemetery.

The dusty cave was surprisingly small and smelt of fish. 'Nothing here!' said Gramps, poking its walls with his walking stick.

But Jasmine looked as well and – hurrah! – there was the next envelope, hanging like a bat above Gramps's head. 'Give it to me ... please,' said Jasmine.

This is somewhere where your wishes may come true, she read.

The next letter of the mystery message was **E**.

Chapter 6

Wishing Tree Wishes

BUMP! Gramps and Jasmine landed in front of a banyan tree in Lam Tsuen. On a rack nearby, hundreds of red wishing slips fluttered in the breeze.

'Here's ten dollars,' said Gramps.

Jasmine ran to a stall to buy cards that could be thrown up onto the wishing tree. Each card had a piece of string and a plastic orange attached to it. With her thick black-ink pen, she wrote: *I wish I could eat–*

Gramps pointed to another banyan tree.

'Which one is the wishing tree?' he asked. Surely *that* one wasn't real. The bark felt cold, lifeless. 'Plastic,' said Jasmine, frowning.

'The original wishing tree is the camphor tree. The second one is a banyan which caught fire, the third is plastic, and a fourth was donated in 2008,' she read from her app. 'This must be the third,' she said.

Fortunately, there was a map and a friendly guide explained. 'You can only throw your wish on the plastic one,' he said. 'Too many wishes have damaged the first and second.'

Gramps was looking dreamy. 'The last time I was here, Nai Nai and I wished your mama a healthy baby: you,' he said. 'I tied our wishing card to a real orange, threw it as high as I could, and guess what happened?'

Jasmine rolled her eyes. 'It landed on your head?'

Historical Site 6: *The Lam Tsuen Wishing Tree*

Gramps laughed and Jasmine glowed inside. Perhaps she should write a wish for him, her parents too. She finished her sentence with the words – *chicken wings* and on a new line added: *I wish Gramps, Ma and Pa will always be healthy.*

Gramps wrote two wishes. One, that Nai Nai was happy in heaven and two, that Jasmine would be a good student. They took photos of all the trees, and the toilet building, which looked more like a temple than a WC.

What a fun day! Even the sun was smiling. But where could the next envelope be? Smoke curled from incense sticks near a cluster of Buddha statues. Red lanterns rocked. Love locks tinkled. There was something white tucked between a stone elephant and a vase. Jasmine ran over to it.

The clue was: *It is fired every day at noon.*

The next letter of the mystery message was **Y**.

Chapter 7

A Dragon's Cannon

Jasmine woke to the sound of birds. She'd missed saying goodbye to her parents, again. Gramps was sitting in his armchair watching the news. 'If we get the MTR directly to Causeway Bay we can eat some yum-yum *dim sum* for breakfast,' she said.

Gramps slapped his hand against the arm rest. 'Good deal,' he said. Which is how, this trip, Jasmine could explore the tunnel leading to the Noonday Gun, and Gramps could eat his favourite *hau gao*.

Jasmine did some research on her app while waiting for the trolley ladies to bring her favourite toffee bananas: *In the early colonial days, Jardine Matheson's main offices and godowns were here. A private army guarded the area. Whenever a big boss came to Hong Kong, soldiers saluted him with a firing of the gun. The Japanese stole it during the Occupation but after the war, a new one was made. Since then the gun is fired every day at noon. It's also fired on the stroke of midnight of New Year's Day.*

Chomped shrimps rolled round Gramps's mouth like clothes in a washing machine. 'When we used to bring you here for lunch as a baby, Nai Nai and I played a game with you,' he said. 'A minute before the gun fired, she'd say, 'Eat up, or the sky dragon will send a clap of thunder.' He flashed his correct-to-the-sec-

Historical Site 7: The Noon Day Gun

ond watch. 'Ten seconds before noon, if there was still rice in your bowl, I would call out the last five seconds: 5, 4, 3, 2, 1 ... BOOM!'

Jasmine made her funny face. Tricked, as usual!

The tunnel to the gun was dark and dank, but had signposts that led them under the rumbling highway. Jasmine lent Gramps a shoulder to help him climb the steps to the quay. It was just before noon.

Oh no! The gun was covered by a green tarpaulin. 'To stop dust jamming its insides, I suppose,' grumbled Gramps.

There was noisy building work all around them. Loud grinding sounds grated. Huge cranes lifted slabs of concrete. Jasmine sighed. She looked out to the sea. Sampans, like sea beetles with sore throats, chugged to and fro. At least the nine sleeping dragon mountains of Kowloon looked peaceful. And silvery fish darted in the harbour.

Jasmine put her matching cap on. She closed her eyes, imagined throwing off the green tarpaulin, pulling the trigger and – BOOM! – blasting it skywards.

Gramps was poking his stick underneath it. 'Take a peep,' he said.

Jasmine peered inside but couldn't see a

thing. *Aargh,* what was that? A bat? She ducked her head as something brushed her cheek. On no, thank goodness. It was the envelope. Gramps chuckled.

Jasmine couldn't help laughing too. She tore open the envelope and eagerly read the contents inside: *'To this day, a place of Christian worship.'*

The mystery letter was **O**.

Chapter 8

A Place of Worship

'Where were you yesterday?' said Mr Crewman. He wasn't smiling.

'Sorry!' said Jasmine, blushing.

'All my fault,' said Gramps.

Mr Crewman flashed his gold teeth. 'No worries, my friends,' he said, reaching for their capsule.

There was a rushing, a sucking, a watery WHOOSH – and they'd arrived. Jasmine read about St. John's Cathedral: *Built between 1847 and 1849. Shaped like a cross. One of the oldest cathedrals in Asia.*

The building resembled a royal castle. Tall towers and turrets, pointed window frames, and window blinds like angels' wings. Ahead, in the dim light, glowed a silver font of holy water. 'Nai Nai used to worship here when she was a girl,' whispered Gramps.

To enter, they had to walk across a mosaic of a mad-eyed eagle. Jasmine shook inside. Its claws looked like they could slice her skin to shreds.

Ceiling fans cooled the wooden pews. Gramps lowered his head to pray. Jasmine could guess who for. She closed her eyes and said a little prayer for Nai Nai too. She waited patiently for Gramps to finish. On a bright stained-glass window above, Jesus hung from a cross. How painful his death must have been. Was it God or the shadows of swaying trees that made it look as if he were moving?

Singers filed in the choir stalls, flicked on red lamps, and opened their folders. A bell chimed. Visitors had to leave. Gramps was still praying. Jasmine nudged him and he nudged her back.

Then the organ was playing and the singers were *la-la-la-ing*. But Jasmine and Gramps hadn't hadn't even started looking for the next clue!

On their way out, they looked from pew to pew. Was it behind that statue or was it in the pulpit? Oh dear, it could be anywhere.

Goodness me! There was an envelope hidden beneath the font. Was it there before? Jasmine didn't think so. She opened the envelope and silently read the next clue: *'The place where Carrie Lam lives.'*

'And what's the next letter?' asked Gramps.

Historical Site 8: St. John's Cathedral

It was **U**.

Chapter 9

Saved by the CE

'The Ferris wheel *spins* you there?' Ma choked on her morning tea.

Gramps shrugged. 'It's a mystery,' he said, winking at Jasmine.

Pa turned a page of his newspaper. 'You've still got ten sites left? You'd better get going, Ferris wheel or no Ferris wheel.'

Yep. Ten sites in ten days. Then back to school. Jasmine couldn't wait to talk to Teacher Tam.

Eiya! The gates of Government House

were guarded by a policewoman with a gun. And the spikes on top of the walls would impale any intruder. Jasmine read from her app: *The official residence of Hong Kong's Chief Executive, built in 1855.*

A sweeping driveway led to a front door and flowering bushes. Jasmine imagined herself hiding behind one to play peek-a-boo with all the fine people who visited.

Crackle crackle. The policewoman's walkie-talkie came to life. 'Move to the side, please,' she said. Gramps stood to attention on the pavement. *Flap flap* went the flag on the bonnet of the approaching car. Someone was winding down a back window. It was Carrie Lam, smiling and waving!

Beep. Beep. The policewoman's telephone buzzed. She pressed its screen. 'Good morning, Ma'am ... Yes? Why yes!' She turned sharply, marched towards a sentry box, reappeared with an envelope and handed it to Jasmine.

'Thank you.' Jasmine ran her fingers over the neatly-written characters of her Chinese name.

'Delivered over a week or so ago,' said the policewoman, jangling her keys. 'I was going to throw it away but Mrs Lam suggested I keep it.'

The clue was in two parts, one Chinese and one English:

i) *A grade-one listed tong lau,* and:

ii) *Roses are red, Violets are ____. You're well on your way and good luck to you.*

What were violets? Jasmine had to Google for a Chinese translation. She thought of colour words that rhymed with the word 'you'.

The next letter of the mystery message was **H**.

Historical Site 9: Government House

Chapter 10

Feeling Blue in Wan Chai

Blue, that was the colour! Jasmine tried to remember blue places in Hong Kong. But all that came to mind was her exercise book, her crayon and a T-shirt.

Gramps was snoozing in his armchair. No help at all.

Jasmine Googled *blue things in Hong Kong* and got her answer: *The Blue House, a museum of storytelling. The four-storey Lingnan-style house was built in the 1920s with both Chinese and Western architectural features.*

Gramps changed into his outdoor shoes and packed his umbrella in his backpack. 'If we're going to Wan Chai, I'd like to buy some egg tarts,' he said.

'I'd prefer a lollipop please,' said Jasmine. They were already on Stone Nullah Lane and Jasmine chose one that matched her hair. She licked it all the way past colourful toy shops and hawkers' stalls in Wan Chai Market. Where was the house? There it was: across the road. Unmistakeable. The bluest house you can imagine. But it looked oh-so closed with its metal gates, bamboo scaffolding, padlocks and metal bars. Wasn't it a museum? Jasmine was looking forward to listening to stories. 'Closed for renovation,' said a worker.

Where could the next envelope be? Jasmine threw her lolly stick in a bin and started looking. She scanned the tiled roof, and spotted two ceramic fish.

'Well I never,' said Gramps as one of the fish gasped to life and flipped an envelope from its fin tail. The envelope sailed down towards them like a yacht.

Jasmine caught it and ripped the envelope open.

The clue was: *'A memorial gate which leads to one of the oldest zoological and botanical gardens in the world.'* Easy! Jasmine knew where they had to travel the next day.

Gramps tweaked the long, curly hair that grew from a mole below his lip. 'Give me another clue,' he said.

Jasmine shook her head while making a note of the next letter.

It was the letter **A**.

Historical Site 10: The Blue House

Chapter 11

A Peaceful Haven

'Capsule number eight, all yours,' said Mr Crewman, and winked.

'Quickly, Gramps,' said Jasmine. Rain clouds were spitting rain and Gramps was plastering her legs with mosquito repellent.

Jasmine and Gramps entered the familiar capsule. Rush, suck, slobbery WHOOSH and they'd landed at the Hong Kong Zoological and Botanical Gardens in Central. *One of the oldest in the world,* Jasmine read from her app. *Magnificent flora when in bloom. Enjoy magnolias, azaleas, bauhinias, bamboo.*

Gramps was smelling a camellia bush. 'Nai Nai's favourite,' he said, and sighed.

In a nearby pond, an elegant pink bird stood one-legged, pecking insects. 'It's called a flamingo,' said Jasmine. *Hoot hoot*, agreed an orang-utan swinging on a branch in its cage.

'Wow! I don't believe it. It says there are six hundred different types of birds here, as well as seventy mammals and forty reptiles.'

'Seeing is believing,' said Gramps.

True. Jasmine didn't spot the lemurs, snakes and turtles. But looking down towards Government House, she espied an elegant arch. The words inscribed on it read, *In memory of the Chinese who died loyal to the Allied cause in the Wars.*

'Nai Nai often went hungry during the war,' said Gramps. Which war was that? Jasmine did some maths, not her best subject, to work it out. As Hong Kong History Girl, she knew that World War I was from 1914 to 1918 and World War II was from 1939 to 1945. Nai Nai had been seventy-eight when she died. 'The Second World War?' she asked.

Gramps nodded. 'While I was riding buffaloes in the rice fields in Guangdong.'

Skipping down the stairs, Jasmine spotted more evidence that Hong Kong was once a British colony: there was a statue of George VI, a king of England. '*Erected in 1942 when Hong Kong had been a British colony for one hundred years,*' she read from her app. She imagined being so famous that a statue was made of her one day.

One of the lions guarding the arch held an envelope under its paw. Jasmine unfolded the paper inside. The clue was: *Only four of these*

Historical Site 11: Hong Kong Zoological and Botanical Gardens

are left in Hong Kong. They are so close you could walk there right now.

'I know, I know,' she cried, pulling Gramps's skinny arm.

It had been spotting rain since morning. Now a raincloud burst. *Croak croak* sang frogs from the drains.

'Get my umbrella out,' said Gramps, hurriedly making a note of the mystery letter.

It was the letter **D**.

Chapter 12

Lit up by Lamplight

Jasmine used a map app to find the way to the Duddell Street gas lamps. Fortunately Jasmine's favourite trainers hadn't gotten too wet in the rain. It was already late afternoon and the sun slipped behind Sunset Peak.

Ding. Her phone beeped. It was Mum. *'Don't make Gramps too tired, History Girl,'* she'd texted. Well, Gramps was shaking his umbrella. He still looked lively to her.

Jasmine read him what Wiki said about Ice House Street on her phone: *'This is where all*

Hong Kong's imported ice used to be stored before there was refrigeration. An airport-sized building would be needed to keep enough ice for today's population!'

Ice House Street gradually wound down to Duddell Street. *'George Duddell was a landowner in the 1870s,'* read Jasmine.

'Are you sure we're walking in the right direction?' said Gramps.

They were, because ahead Jasmine spotted two of the four lampposts. When she screwed her eyes up they looked like farmers wearing big straw hats in paddy fields.

The other two lampposts were at the bottom of a stone staircase. Jasmine stepped forward to take a photo, when – *flick!* – the lamps lit up. It was exactly six o'clock.

'In the olden days, the lamps were lit by a man with a long rod,' said Gramps, reading from a plaque. The lamplight cast long shadows on the stairs. Jasmine imagined how pretty Hong Kong must have looked when only gas lamps lit the city.

Now where was the next envelope? Holding hands, Jasmine and Gramps slowly walked down the steps, scanning the balustrades.

No luck. Had someone found it and taken it away? Maybe it had been swept away by street sweepers. Heavy-hearted, Jasmine waited while Gramps caught his breath to climb back up the stone staircase. 'We can't give up now,' he said.

Jasmine peeked behind the nearest pillar. And there it was, hidden between a gas container and the stone wall. The clue was: *The oldest market structure in the city.*

The next letter of the mystery message was **S**.

Historical Site 12: Duddell Street Gas Lamps

Chapter 13

A Fairytale Market

The Hong Kong Ferris wheel shone silver in the sun, its spindly spokes spinning the capsules to who knows where. A tent shaped like a giant white cockroach bulged in the breeze. Jasmine hadn't noticed it before. Was that where Mr Crewman lived?

He seemed to come alive as they approached. Doffing his cap and said, 'Do you know where you're going this fine morning?'

'I'm afraid—' Gramps didn't finish. Mr Crewman had raised his walkie-talkie and was shouting, 'Number eight!'

Like magic, the whirring wheel slowed, the capsule door clunked opened, and Jasmine hopped into its cool interior.

How quickly they climbed. *Wheeee!*

Western Market, in Sheung Wan. A tram trundled past and Jasmine imagined taking photos of the fine old building from the upper floor. She read from her app: *'The market first opened for business in 1844.'*

'Your great-great grandparents may have shopped here,' said Gramps, tapping his walking stick on the pavement.

A life-size toy soldier stood to attention at the main entrance. 'Excuse me, have you seen an envelope addressed for me?' asked Jasmine jokingly.

The soldier creaked and marched towards a bright red telephone box!

'Wah!' said Gramps.

The soldier shook its head and pointed to the grand stairway leading upwards.

Jasmine and Gramps were so excited they barely glanced at a doll's house version of the market. They ignored model train engines, jewels, treasures, toys. The first floor was like a giant den draped with rolls and rolls of exotic fabrics. The second floor was like a fairyland with sparkling chandeliers and spotlights shimmering like frozen rain. There was a wedding party in full swing there, with a musician tinkling piano keys and a singer moving her hips in time with the music. Hundreds of guests sat around tables draped in white silk, clinking glasses, laughing. People had to register with a lady at the entrance. She looked like she'd stepped out of Gramps's Qing dynasty book of Eastern beauties. 'I don't think

Historical Site 13: Western Market

we're invited,' he whispered.

'What's your name, dear?' asked the painted lady. 'Yes, you are! Well your granddaughter is.' She handed Jasmine an envelope.

It wasn't an invitation. Inside there was a piece of paper with the clue: *People have checked the time here since 1915.*

The mystery letter was **O**.

Chapter 14

A Clock Marks the Spot

The walls of the Kowloon-Canton Railway tower vibrated with the *tick-tick-tocking* of the clock. 'This place has special memories for me,' said Gramps. '1972, that's the year I arrived from China, with nothing but a pair of shorts and flip-flops.' He closed his eyes and breathed deeply. 'I can still smell the roasting chicken wings. But they were twenty cents each and I only had five in my pocket.'

Jasmine touched the warm baked bricks of the tower. How many joyful family reunions had taken place here? She imagined trains blasting clouds of steam, the bustle of weary travellers spilling from carriages. *It took three whole years to complete the original station,* she read from her app. *It opened for business in 1915 and was demolished in 1975. Some people wanted the clock tower to be knocked down too but others campaigned hard to keep it. Eventually the history-lovers won.* 'Let's climb the spiral stairs to the top,' she said.

Gramps gripped her arm. 'Not permitted anymore,' he said. 'but I remember Nai Nai telling me she did so once as a teenager. In the belfry there's a bell, but it hasn't rung for years.'

Jasmine found some shade and sketched the tower in her notebook. Turrets, buttresses, and cornices. She'd studied some architectural words and wanted to add examples of them in her project.

Gramps was still daydreaming about Nai Nai. 'She told me the clock only stopped once,' he said. 'It was during the Japanese Occupation. When the arms of the clock froze, it seemed the whole world had come to a standstill.'

On the other side of the harbour the Ferris wheel sparkled like morning dew on a spider's web. It was getting late and they hadn't started looking for the envelope. Jasmine found it wedged in a crack in the tower wall. The clue was: *A Taoist temple where the Secretary of Home Affairs picks a fortune stick on Chinese New Year's Day.*

The next letter of the mystery message was **M**.

Historical Site 14: Kowloon-Canton Railways Clock Tower

Chapter 15

Fortune Telling

There were only four more days left of the summer holiday. Jasmine imagined Teacher Tam slapping a super-sized gold star on her classroom wall chart. Her history project had gone so well and had been so exciting. And what were the last four letters of the secret message IHOPEYOUHADSOM? She couldn't wait to find out.

'Me too,' said Gramps.

One swing of the Ferris wheel and they'd landed at the entrance of Wong Tai Sin Temple.

Smoke curled from the incense sticks of roadside stalls. They took a few photos then followed the crowd past two fierce dragons and statues of Chinese zodiac animals. Jasmine read from her app: '*This Taoist temple became popular from 1915 when a Chinese medicine man opened a shop with an image of the Taoist god of healing, Wong Tai Sin. Today many people come here to pray.*'

Gramps stood beside a shrine for a land god. 'Home is where the heart is,' he said. The adjacent shrine, a money god's, was also buzzing with people bowing and praying.

Inside the main temple, a monk beat a drum while chanting. Ladies lowered plates of fruit in reverence to Wong Tai Sin. The smoky air made Jasmine's eyes water.

An old woman was kneeling on a cushion shaking *kau cim* sticks. 'How about I get a clue for the clue by shaking some myself?' said Jasmine.

'Good idea,' said Gramps

The tumbler of sticks felt light. Jasmine shook it and all the sticks jumped forward. 'Slowly,' said Gramps.

At last, number seventeen slid out. Jasmine ran over to a stand to select the fortune-poem of that number.

'I can interpret that for you,' called a wrinkled fortune-teller with goggle-sized glasses from a nearby stall. Jasmine pulled Gramps towards him.

The fortune-teller twitched his long beard and scratched his head. 'I think it's telling me that you are the owner of this,' he said, reaching for an envelope under his desk.

The clue was: *A place between Statue Square and City Hall which honours the dead.*

Historical Site 15: Wong Tai Sin Temple

‘What, *another* war memorial?’ said Jasmine.

Gramps twitched his eyebrows.

The next letter of the mystery message was **E**.

Chapter 16

Bravery Rewarded

'I think Teacher Tam chose another war memorial because he wants us to remember the brave people who sacrificed their lives for Hong Kong,' said Gramps. He was stirring Chinese medicine in the kitchen. Jasmine's bedroom, the bathroom, the whole flat, stank of it. 'Let's go!' said Jasmine.

Under the scorching sun, Mr Crewman looked rather fuzzy around the edges. 'Hardly worth spinning you there,' he said.

The monument looked lonely standing in

the middle of a grass lawn. Chains surrounded the area so Jasmine didn't dare to approach it. 'Do you think there are soldiers buried underneath?' she said.

Gramps tapped the pavement with his walking stick. 'I thought I heard something,' he said.

Jasmine read from her app: *The Cenotaph commemorates fallen soldiers in World Wars One and Two. Local Chinese, Indian, Nepalese and British soldiers fought to save Hong Kong. Some served in the Royal Navy, others in the British Army and the Royal Air Force. Hongkongers were on the Allied side and were finally victorious.*

'Excuse me,' said Jasmine. A suited man was carrying two flower wreaths. Jasmine read one of the labels. *To Sergeant CK Wong. Your bravery will never be forgotten.* The roses smelled sweet as jam. She moved aside as the man unhooked the chain. Hey, was that an envelope lodged between two flowers?

'Are you Miss Jasmine?' said the man, passing her the envelope.

The next clue read: '*I sail on the sea. Add a C and my English name could be the name for a baby duck.*'

'No idea,' said Gramps.

Jasmine burst out laughing. 'I know! I studied it in my last history project. *Duk Ling*. It's the name of a famous junk. Haven't you seen it sailing round the harbour?'

Gramps shook his head.

The next letter of the mystery message was **F**.

Historical Site 16: The Cenotaph

Chapter 17

More and More Magical

'Good morning, I was expecting you,' said Mr Crewman.

He reached for the lever above the door of capsule eight and clamped it shut.

'Wait!' said Gramps. Too late, they were already climbing.

Jasmine laughed. Gramps couldn't swim so she knew what was worrying him. He didn't want to land in the sea.

But if the truth be known, she was a bit worried too. Where was the junk now? She knelt on the capsule bench to get a better view of the harbour. There it was! Near the Cultural Centre. Its distinctive brown sails flapped in the wind.

Up went their capsule, rocking to and fro, a little too fast for comfort, then a high-pitched beep, a stomach-churning lurch and they'd landed on the afterdeck. Fortunately no tourists noticed. *Squawk squawk!* A surprised seagull flew from the mast.

Jasmine read from her app: *Duk Ling junk. Built in 1955 in Macau. The last authentic junk in Hong Kong. Modelled on junks built in the Qing dynasty.* She imagined herself in the olden days, a fine lady dressed in silk, jewelled pins in her thick black hair, fluttering a fan.

What beautiful views! From right to left, all the way round, buildings glinted in the sun. Jasmine wished her history project would never end. The rocking of the boat lulled her into a peaceful dream of seeing Teacher Tam's smile as she handed him the finished project.

A huge hawk was circling the boat. Jasmine shaded her eyes to look at it. What was that in its beak? An envelope! It fluttered through the air and landed on the deck. Teacher Tam's magic was more mysterious by the day.

'I thought it dropped something else,' said Gramps, laughing.

Teacher Tam's magic was getting more magic by the day.

The clue was: *This park was a walled city from the fifteenth century.*

The seventeenth letter was **U**.

After they docked Gramps took a photo of Jasmine and the junk.

Historical Site 17: Duk Ling Junk

Chapter 18

A Fantastical Journey Ends

'Why is he sending you there?' said Mr Crewman. 'Kowloon Walled City was knocked down decades ago.'

'When can we meet again?' said Jasmine.

'Goodbye my friends,' said Mr Crewman.

Why was he smiling when this was their last trip?

'It's been a pleasure,' said Gramps.

As the capsule climbed, Jasmine waved. And then gasped. In front of her eyes, the man with the gold teeth was melting like butter left out of the fridge for too long.

Rush, suck, watery WHOOSH and they'd landed in a park.

Trees rustled in a gentle breeze. Birds tweeted. It was so peaceful compared to Central. Jasmine read from her app: ... *originally a Chinese military fort. When the British leased the New Territories in 1898, they weren't allowed to govern the walled city and it gradually became a haven for crime and drugs.* Jasmine imagined tattooed men making mysterious signs with chopped fingers, the clanging and whirring of small workshops, foul smells. Now they were surrounded by pretty pavilions and neat gardens.

'I saw the city being demolished with my own eyes,' said Gramps. 'It was around 1994, if I remember correctly.'

In the museum in the heart of the park

there was a miniature model of the bustling Qing dynasty village of old. *A Chinese official lived here right up until 1899*, Jasmine read from her app. She sketched an image of his *yamen*.

The sun dipped behind a cloud. It was getting late. An evening breeze ruffled Jasmine's sketchbook. The following morning school term would begin. She had never realised Hong Kong had such a fascinating history. Thanks to Teacher Tam for planning such a fantastic project! Thanks to Gramps for coming with her! Look how his eyes sparkled. He'd had some fun too. She hugged him.

'How about an ice-cream?' he said.

Now where was that last envelope? They needed proof of the last letter, even though Jasmine felt sure she knew what it would be. They were staring down at two giant boulders,

Historical Site 18: Kowloon Walled City

left where archaeologists had found them while digging. The broken one had the four characters of the old city inscribed on it.

'I think I can see it,' said Gramps excitedly.

Sure enough, tucked in a fissure, fluttered an envelope.

The paper inside was folded in four. There was no clue, of course. Jasmine made her funny face.

But there was the very last letter. She'd guessed correctly.

It was the letter **N**.

Now you have finished reading Jasmine's magical adventure.

What is the secret message?

Write it down here.

THE END

English-Chinese Names of the Historical Sites Jasmine Visited

Chapter 1

Sung Wong Toi 宋王臺

Chapter 2

Man Cheong Pagoda文昌塔

Chapter 3

Tang Chung Ling Ancestral Hall 松嶺鄧公祠

Chapter 4

Fan Lau Fort 分流炮台

Chapter 5

Cheung Po Tsai's Cave 張保仔洞

Chapter 6

The Lam Tsuen Wishing Tree 林村許願樹

Chapter 7

The Noon Day Gun 怡和午炮

Chapter 8

St. John's Cathedral 聖約翰座堂

Chapter 9

Government House 禮賓府

Chapter 10

The Blue House 藍屋

Chapter 11

Hong Kong Zoological and Botanical Gardens
香港動植物公園

Chapter 12

Duddell Street Gas Lamps 都爹利街石階煤氣燈

Chapter 13

Western Market 西港城

Chapter 14

Kowloon-Canton Railway Clock Tower 前九廣鐵路鐘樓

Chapter 15

Wong Tai Sin Temple 黃大仙祠

Chapter 16

The Cenotaph 和平紀念碑

Chapter 17

Duk Ling Junk 鴨靈號帆船

Chapter 18

Kowloon Walled City 九龍寨城

Useful Websites for You to Discover More About Hong Kong

Like Jasmine in the story, you can visit historical sites and study some history. Here are some useful websites for your reference. Enjoy!

1 **Sung Wong Toi**
https://commons.wikimedia.org/wiki/Category:Sung_Wong_Toi
http://www.mtr.com.hk/en/customer/tourist/myitinerary5.php?attId=197

2 **Man Cheong Pagoda**
http://www.amo.gov.hk/form/ytsh_201611.pdf

3 **Tang Chung Ling Ancestral Hall**
https://en.wikipedia.org/wiki/Tang_Chung_Ling_Ancestral_Hall

4 Fan Lau Fort

https://commons.wikimedia.org/wiki/Category:Fan_Lau_Fort

5 Cheung Po Tsai's Cave

http://www.discoverhongkong.com/nz/see-do/culture-heritage/historical-sites/chinese/cheung-po-tsai-cave.jsp

6 The Lam Tsuen Wishing Tree

https://en.wikipedia.org/wiki/Lam_Tsuen_wishing_trees
http://www.discoverhongkong.com/nz/see-do/culture-heritage/historical-sites/chinese/lam-tsuen-wishing-tree.jsp

7 The Noon Day Gun

https://en.wikipedia.org/wiki/Noonday_Gun
http://www.discoverhongkong.com/nz/see-do/culture-heritage/historical-sites/colonial/noon-day-gun.jsp

8 St. John's Cathedral

http://www.stjohnscathedral.org.hk/Index.aspx
http://www.amo.gov.hk/en/monuments_60.php
http://www.discoverhongkong.com/nz/see-do/cul-

ture-heritage/other-places-of-worship/st-john-cathedral.jsp

9 Government House

http://www.discoverhongkong.com/nz/see-do/culture-heritage/historical-sites/colonial/government-house.jsp

10 The Blue House

https://www.scmp.com/news/hong-kong/community/article/2117982/hong-kongs-historic-blue-house-wins-unescos-highest

http://www.discoverhongkong.com/nz/see-do/culture-heritage/historical-sites/colonial/the-blue-house.jsp

11 Hong Kong Zoological and Botanical Gardens

https://www.lcsd.gov.hk/en/parks/hkzbg/

http://www.discoverhongkong.com/uk/see-do/great-outdoors/city-parks/zoological-and-botanical-gardens.jsp

12 Duddell Street Gas Lamps

https://en.wikipedia.org/wiki/Duddell_Street

https://industrialhistoryhk.org/dudell-street-gas-lamps/

http://www.discoverhongkong.com/uk/see-do/culture-heritage/historical-sites/colonial/duddell-street-steps.jsp

13 Western Market

https://westernmarket.com.hk/
http://www.discoverhongkong.com/uk/shop/where-to-shop/malls-and-department-stores/western-market.jsp

14 Kowloon-Canton Railway Clock Tower

http://www.amo.gov.hk/en/monuments_43.php
http://www.discoverhongkong.com/uk/see-do/highlight-attractions/top-10/clock-tower.jsp

15 Wong Tai Sin Temple

http://www.discoverhongkong.com/uk/see-do/culture-heritage/chinese-temples/wong-tai-sin-temple.jsp
http://www1.siksikyuen.org.hk/en/wong-tai-sin-temple

16 The Cenotaph

https://en.wikipedia.org/wiki/The_Cenotaph_(Hong_Kong)
https://commons.wikimedia.org/wiki/Category:Cenotaph,_Hong_Kong

17 Duk Ling Junk

https://www.scmp.com/photos/today-photos/gallery/1779731/return-clever-duck-junk-hong-kong-harbour

http://www.discoverhongkong.com/uk/see-do/tours-walks/guided-tours/victoria-harbour/dukling-harbour-cruise.jsp

18 Kowloon Walled City

https://www.scmp.com/news/hong-kong/article/1191748/kowloon-walled-city-life-city-darkness

http://www.discoverhongkong.com/uk/see-do/culture-heritage/historical-sites/chinese/kowloon-walled-city-park.jsp

Your Notes

Like Jasmine in the story, jot down notes about each historical site.

Write the name of the historical site.

Describe how you got there.

Describe what impressed you most at the historical site.

Describe how you felt during your visit.

Take a photo and make a sketch of it.

Write the name of the historical site.

Describe how you got there.

Describe what impressed you most at the historical site.

Describe how you felt during your visit.

Take a photo and make a sketch of it.

Colour it

Hong Kong Zoological and Botanical Gardens

Duddell Street Gas Lamps